America's Leaders

The White House Press Secretary

by Joanne Mattern

BLACKBIRCH® PRESS

San Diego • Detroit • New York • San Francisco • Cleveland • New Haven, Conn. • Waterville, Maine • London • Munich

© 2003 by Blackbirch Press™. Blackbirch Press™ is an imprint of The Gale Group, Inc., a division of Thomson Learning, Inc.

Blackbirch Press™ and Thomson Learning™ are trademarks used herein under license.

For more information, contact
The Gale Group, Inc.
27500 Drake Rd.
Farmington Hills, MI 48331-3535
Or you can visit our Internet site at http://www.gale.com

ALL RIGHTS RESERVED
No part of this work covered by the copyright hereon may be reproduced or used in any form or by any means—graphic, electronic, or mechanical, including photocopying, recording, taping, Web distribution or information storage retrieval systems—without the written permission of the publisher.

Every effort has been made to trace the owners of copyrighted material.

Photo credits: Cover, back cover © Creatas; White House cover inset, page 4 © Blackbirch Press Archives; Steven Early cover inset, james Brady cover inset, Ari Fleischer cover inset, pages 8, 9, 10, 11, 12, 13, 14, 15, 16, 17, 18, 20, 21, 22, 23, 24, 25, 26, 27, 28, 29, 30, 32 © CORBIS; pages 6, 7 © Library of Congress; page 18 © National Archives

---

LIBRARY OF CONGRESS CATALOGING-IN-PUBLICATION DATA

Mattern, Joanne, 1963-
 The press secretary / by Joanne Mattern.
     p. cm. — (America's leaders series)
Summary: Takes a thorough look at the President's press secretary, including the history of the office, how the work relates to that of other government offices, and how press secretaries have handled crises.
 ISBN 1-56711-281-1 (hardback : alk. paper)
 1. Presidential press secretaries—United States—Juvenile literature. 2. Presidential press secretaries—United States—History—Juvenile literature. 3. Presidential press secretaries—United States—Biography—Juvenile literature. [1. Presidential press secretaries.] I. Title. II. Series.
 E176.47 .M38 2003
 352.23'2748'0973—dc21   2002011929

Printed in United States
10 9 8 7 6 5 4 3 2 1

Table of Contents

The Voice of the President 4

On the Job 11

Who Works with the Press Secretary? 15

Where Does the Press Secretary Work? 17

Requirements for the Job 20

A Time of Crisis 22

Another Time of Crisis 24

A Press Secretary's Day 26

Fascinating Facts 28

Glossary 30

For More Information 31

Index 32

The Voice of the President

More than 200 years ago, a group of men wrote a document, the U.S. Constitution, which established the American government. The authors of the Constitution split the government into three separate branches. These are the legislative branch, the judicial branch, and the executive branch.

Under the Constitution, the legislative branch was made up of the Senate and the House of Representatives. The judicial branch was the nation's court system, with the Supreme Court as the highest court. The executive branch was led by the president.

The U.S. Constitution was signed in 1787. This document established the three branches of government.

President Dwight D. Eisenhower's press secretary, James Hagerty, held a press conference in Washington, D.C., in 1956.

Many people work for the president. Some advise him and help him make decisions. Others schedule his appointments and public appearances. Many members of the president's staff work behind the scenes. They are seldom known to the public. One member of the president's staff, however, talks to the public and the media every day. He or she gives the nation news about the president. He or she also tells reporters how the president feels about certain issues, and what he plans to do. This person is the press secretary.

Amos Kendall was the private secretary to Andrew Jackson.

> **USA Fact**
> In his later years, Amos Kendall, who was one of President Andrew Jackson's assistants, gave two acres of his land in Washington, D.C., to start a school for deaf and blind children. Over time, the school Kendall helped start became the well-known Gallaudet University.

For most of the history of the United States, presidents did not have official press secretaries. It was not until James Buchanan became president in 1857 that Congress voted to give the president some money to hire a secretary to help him. Before that, presidents used their own money to hire private secretaries. Sometimes, the private secretary's job included answering questions from the press. Some presidents chose friends or former reporters to do this job.

During the first 100 years of American history, the news media was not as interested in the president's activities and opinions as it is today. Instead, reporters concentrated more on what Congress and other government officials did. There were also fewer news outlets, since radio, television, and the Internet had not yet been invented. Newspapers and magazines were the major sources of news. Some presidents, such as Abraham Lincoln, met informally with a reporter to go over the news of the day. After Lincoln's assassination, his successor, Andrew Johnson, was the first president to give formal newspaper interviews.

By 1896, reporters regularly wrote stories about the president. Soon, reporters were assigned specifically to the White House. These journalists became the first White House press corps.

In the 1800s, people depended on newspapers and magazines to find out the latest news about the government.

The presidents' private secretaries continued to be the official representatives to the press corps until Franklin Roosevelt took office in 1932. Roosevelt asked Stephen T. Early, a reporter, to be his official contact with the press. Instead of carrying the title "private secretary," Early's position had a new title. He was known as the press secretary. Early took the job. He scheduled two press conferences a week, one on Wednesday mornings and one on Friday afternoons.

Unlike earlier secretaries, Early worked actively to get Roosevelt ready for press conferences. The two met

> **USA Fact**
> Stephen T. Early's salary was $9,500 a year.

Stephen T. Early (seated, left) was the first person to have the title of press secretary.

President Franklin D. Roosevelt (seated, right) held his first press conference in 1933.

frequently to talk about news. Early told the president what questions he thought reporters would ask, and suggested answers. Early made copies of important presidential speeches and announcements and gave them out to reporters before a press conference. This way, they would have the actual text to quote in their news stories.

USA Fact
During his first term of office, Roosevelt held 337 press conferences.

Roosevelt's press conferences took place in an office that held about 275 people. The small room was very crowded. All the reporters had to stand, and no cameras or recording devices were allowed in the room.

President Richard Nixon posed with the Washington House Press Corps in Washington, D.C.

Roosevelt soon realized that a more comfortable room was needed. When the West Wing of the White House was enlarged in 1934, Roosevelt had the pressroom made bigger. He also had tables and chairs put in for reporters.

Since Roosevelt's time, press briefings have become larger and more organized.

USA Fact

It was not until February 8, 1944, that the first African American reporter was allowed to attend a White House press conference. The reporter, Harry S. McAlpin, worked for the National Negro Press Association and the *Atlanta Daily World* newspaper.

Today, the White House press corps consists of hundreds of reporters from newspapers, magazines, radio and television networks, and Internet news sources. Many of these people report only on the president and his actions.

On the Job

The press secretary's main job is to be the voice of the president. It is up to him or her to make sure the president's plans, opinions, and feelings are presented accurately to the public.

To keep reporters informed, the press secretary holds daily briefings. During these briefings, the secretary reads statements that outline the president's views on major issues. The secretary may, for example, talk about the president's plans in a financial or military crisis. Other times, the secretary discusses more personal matters, such as the president's health or family issues. Presidents often prefer not to talk about personal matters. In these cases, the press secretary will issue a general statement that has few specific details. In times of crisis, the press secretary may speak to reporters several times a day. He or she may also give out written statements that express the president's opinions or plans.

Press Secretary Pierre Salinger kept reporters informed of President John F. Kennedy's travel plans.

President John F. Kennedy delivered his second press conference on February 1, 1961. Press secretary Pierre Salinger (seated second from right, onstage) organized the press conference.

Press secretaries also run press conferences. At these meetings, the press secretary usually reads a prepared statement. Then he or she answers questions from reporters. Sometimes, the president or chief of staff, rather than the press secretary, will speak to reporters. In these cases, it is the press secretary's job to organize the press conference. The secretary chooses which reporters will ask questions, and makes sure everything runs smoothly.

> **USA Fact**
> John F. Kennedy was the first president to use frequent live press conferences on television as a way to communicate directly with the people. He served as president from 1961 to 1963.

The press secretary's job is challenging. The secretary works long hours. He or she often has to travel with the president or attend meetings with him and other members of the administration. If the press secretary is at home when something newsworthy happens, he or she might be called in the middle of the night. Then he or she must rush to the White House and get to work. During a national crisis, the press secretary may have to stay at the White House all day and all night.

The press secretary also faces a huge amount of pressure. The secretary must stay calm as he or she faces tough questions from the media. He or she must represent the president fairly, yet also be open and helpful to reporters. Some press secretaries have become angry or frustrated because they felt the president and his staff did not give them enough information to do the job well.

President George W. Bush (left) walks with Press Secretary Ari Fleischer. The press secretary often travels with the president.

Sometimes, the press secretary can even face a crisis about the news he or she reports. On August 8, 1974, President Richard Nixon resigned because of his involvement in a series of events known as the Watergate scandal. Nixon's vice president, Gerald Ford, became president. He hired a reporter named Jerry terHorst to be his press secretary.

President Gerald Ford at work in the Oval Office. Ford's press secretary resigned from his position shortly after Ford became president.

Less than a month later, on September 7, Ford told terHorst that he planned to pardon Nixon. Ford hoped the pardon would help the country move beyond the scandal. Jerry terHorst did not think Ford had made the right decision, but he arranged for the president to make the announcement. Just an hour before the announcement, however, terHorst resigned from his job. He said that he simply could not make statements that he did not personally support.

Who Works with the Press Secretary?

The press secretary does not do his or her job alone. The president has an entire staff who works in communications. Although the press secretary is the main contact with the press, other people serve as advisers and special consultants.

The press secretary also has several deputy press secretaries. These people help the press secretary carry out his or her duties. At times, a deputy must take over for the press secretary. In 1981, President Ronald Reagan's press secretary, James Brady, was shot in the head when a man tried to kill the president. Reagan was seriously wounded, too. Because the media and the nation wanted news about Reagan's condition, deputy press secretary Larry Speakes gave reporters the latest information.

After James Brady was injured in 1981, Larry Speakes (pictured) took over his duties.

After he left the White House, James Brady (seated, with his wife Sarah) became a strong supporter of gun control.

Speakes served as the unofficial press secretary for several months. Later, it became clear that Brady's injuries would not allow him to return to work. Speakes took over as the president's spokesman.

USA Fact

Although he could not serve actively, James Brady kept the title of press secretary until the end of the Reagan administration in 1989. After he left the White House, he worked hard to get stronger gun laws passed. The Brady Bill that bears his name requires a waiting period and background check for all handgun purchases.

Where Does the Press Secretary Work?

The press secretary has an office in the White House. It is usually close to the offices of the president's advisers and other staff members. This makes it easy for the press secretary to meet with the president, the chief of staff, and other members of the executive branch. Assistants use smaller offices near the press secretary's office.

In addition to the press secretary's office, there is a special room for press conferences. Over the years, conferences have been held in a number of places in the White House. For many years, reporters simply gathered around the desk in the press secretary's office.

James C. Hagerty (pictured) served as President Dwight D. Eisenhower's press secretary.

Press conferences are held in a special room inside the White House.

Then, in 1973, a new briefing room opened. It has sofas and chairs for the reporters, as well as a platform that the secretary speaks from. Sometimes, though, the press secretary gives a briefing outside of the White House.

At the same time that the new briefing room opened, the press also received a new pressroom. It had 40 desks and 12 broadcast cubicles. Reporters use the room as a place to write and send their stories to news services. It is also a good place for reporters to wait for breaking news or announcements.

The president's plane, *Air Force One*, has several conference rooms. Because the press secretary and members of the media often travel with the president, press conferences may be held in one of these rooms.

President Bill Clinton (left) and Press Secretary Jake Siewert (right) held a press conference aboard Air Force One *(above) on January 17, 2001.*

Requirements for the Job

The press secretary gets the job directly from the president. He or she does not need to be approved by Congress or any other member of the government or the president's staff.

Many people who become press secretaries first work for the president's campaign staff. Campaign work gives future press secretaries many opportunities to talk to the media and get to know reporters. They know how the news business works and what journalists need to do their jobs. It is important for the press secretary to work well with reporters. Otherwise, the media may not trust the press secretary or believe what he or she tells them.

Pierre Salinger worked as a press assistant during John F. Kennedy's presidential campaign.

President Ronald Reagan meets with Press Secretary James Brady.

Press secretaries must also have good communication skills, since they talk to the press daily. Writing skills are needed as well, because the press secretary writes the statements that are released to the media.

The press secretary has to get along with the president, too. They usually meet daily, sometimes even several times a day. The press secretary often goes with the president to speaking engagements, meetings, and to other official visits. The president must trust the press secretary to represent him to the press in a fair and honest way.

A Time of Crisis

A press secretary's main job is to speak for the president in public, but sometimes it is even more important for the press secretary to keep a secret. Some information might upset the public or endanger the country or its troops. It is up to the press secretary to make sure such news does not get out.

One of the first times a press secretary's ability to keep secrets was tested was in 1893. President Grover Cleveland had a cancerous tumor in his mouth and had to have an operation. At that time, the United States was in the middle of an economic crisis.

Daniel Lamont (front row, far left) spoke to the press for President Grover Cleveland (center) about his surgery.

Cleveland did not want to appear weak or unable to do his job during this difficult period. He also worried that his political opponents would use any news that he was ill against him.

On July 1, 1893, Cleveland secretly had surgery on a yacht in Long Island Sound. The next day, his private secretary, Daniel Lamont, told reporters that the president was fine and simply had some trouble with his teeth. When a reporter asked if Cleveland had had an operation, Lamont just said, "That is all," and ended the briefing. Almost two months passed before the true story came out in the newspapers. By then, Cleveland's health had improved, and the story of his illness no longer seemed important.

On September 11, 2001, Press Secretary Ari Fleischer held many televised press conferences to keep the public informed of what President George Bush planned to do.

USA Fact

Perhaps the toughest crisis any press secretary has had to face was the terrorist attack on New York City's World Trade Center and Washington, D.C.'s Pentagon on September 11, 2001. Ari Fleischer, press secretary for President George W. Bush, held many press briefings during the weeks after the attacks. He kept the public informed about the damage done in the attacks and about efforts to bring the terrorists to justice.

Another Time of Crisis

The question of how much to tell the press came up again in April 1980. At that time, 53 Americans were being held hostage by militant students in Iran. Many Americans thought the United States should use the armed forces to free the hostages. President Jimmy Carter did not want to do this. Instead, he tried peacefully to convince Iran to let the hostages go. He froze Iranian assets in the United States, so the country could not get to its money. He also asked other governments to help him persuade Iran to free the hostages. None of these efforts worked.

Carter and his advisers came up with a plan to send special soldiers to rescue the hostages. They knew this mission had to be kept secret to give it a chance to work. If the press reported the plan, people in Iran would find out and be able to stop it.

In 1980, students in Washington, D.C., protested the U.S. government's handling of the hostage crisis in Iran.

Press Secretary Jody Powell misled the press about a planned military attack on Iran, because the mission needed to be kept secret.

For months, the president's press secretary, Jody Powell, knew that there was a military plan to rescue the hostages. He even went to meetings at which the plan was discussed. When rumors of the plan began to circulate, Powell told Jack Nelson, bureau chief of the *Los Angeles Times,* that there would be no military action against Iran.

On April 24, eight helicopters headed for Iran. Something went wrong, and two of the helicopters crashed. Eight U.S. servicemen were killed. That night, Powell called Jack Nelson and admitted that he had lied. Nelson said he understood that Powell had lied because "lives were at stake." Although some members of the public were angry about being deceived, most people realized that Powell had to keep the mission a secret to protect the hostages and the soldiers who tried to rescue them.

A Press Secretary's Day

The press secretary's day is usually a nonstop routine of meetings, press briefings, and travel. Here is what a typical day might be like:

6:30 AM	Wakes; showers; dresses; watches television news
7:30 AM	Has breakfast while reading the newspaper
8:30 AM	Arrives at the White House and goes over work in the office
9:30 AM	Meets with the president to discuss a breaking news story
10:15 AM	Briefs the press and answers questions about the news story
12:00 PM	Eats a quick lunch during a meeting with other members of the president's staff
12:30 PM	Attends meeting with the chief of staff
2:30 PM	Returns to the White House, makes phone calls, and writes correspondence
3:30 PM	Briefs the president before the next press conference

President Jimmy Carter (left) walks with Press Secretary Jody Powell (center), and presidential adviser Stuart Eizenstat. The press secretary has many meetings and press conferences each day.

4:00 PM — Holds another press briefing to update breaking news

5:00 PM — Travels by helicopter with the president to a speaking engagement

9:00 PM — Returns to the White House; goes to the office to catch up on paperwork

10:30 PM — Returns home; watches television; prepares for bed

12:00 AM — Bed

Fascinating Facts

Dee Dee Myers, who served under Bill Clinton, was the first woman press secretary. She was also the youngest one, at 31 years old.

Ari Fleischer's first job as George W. Bush's press secretary was to announce his own appointment to members of the press.

Dee Dee Myers

Ari Fleischer

Ron Ziegler

Ron Ziegler, who was press secretary under Richard Nixon, coined the term photo opportunity in 1969. He used it to describe public situations that would show the president at his best.

Marlin Fitzwater was the first press secretary to serve under two consecutive presidents. He was press secretary for both Ronald Reagan and Reagan's successor, George Bush.

Marlin Fitzwater

Glossary

adviser—someone who works closely with a person in power and provides information and suggestions

Air Force One—a jet built especially for the president and his family

brief—to give someone information so that person can do his or her job

campaign—a series of actions, such as speeches and public appearances, done in order to win an election

Congress—the legislative branch of government, made up of the Senate and the House of Representatives

Constitution—the document that set the United States and outlined the principles of the nation

President Lyndon B. Johnson met with Press Secretary Bill Moyers on the south lawn of the White House.

For More Information

Publications

Nelson, W. Dale. *Who Speaks for the President?* Syracuse, NY: Syracuse University Press, 1998.

Web Sites

Press Briefing Archives

www.whitehouse.gov/firstlady

www.whitehouse.gov/news

This official White House site includes transcripts and audio of recent briefings and news conferences given by the press secretary.

Press Secretary Ron Nessen (left) appears in a comedy sketch with comedian Chevy Chase playing President Ford.

Index

Air Force One 19
Brady Bill 16
Branches of the government . .4
Buchanan, James 6
Campaign staff 20
Carter, Jimmy 24–25
Cleveland, Grover 22-23
Constitution 4
Crisis 11, 13, 14
Daily briefings 10

Deputy press secretaries 15
Early, Stephen T. 8-9
Iran, hostage crisis in 24–24
Lincoln, Abraham 7
Los Angeles Times 25
McAlpin, Harry S. 10
News outlets 7
Powell, Jody 25
Pressroom 18
Private secretaries 6, 8

Reagan, Ronald 15, 16, 21
Roosevelt, Franklin 8–9
Running a press conference . .12
Speakes, Larry 15–16
Supreme Court 4
terHorst, Jerry 14
Watergate 14
West Wing, the 10
White House press corps . .7, 10